DATE DUE

DEC 0 1 1997			

RETURN

OF THE

WOLF

RETURN
OF THE
WOLF

By

Dorothy Hinshaw Patent

Illustrated by
Jared Taylor Williams

Clarion Books/*New York*

I want to thank Pat Tucker, Roland Smith, Greg Patent, Jason Patent, and Deborah Bond for their helpful comments on the manuscript, and Dorothy Briley for having the faith in me to publish this book, my first fiction story. Thanks also go to the canines in my life who have inspired me—Koani, Elsa, Ninja, and the residents of Wolf Scat Ranch. Most of all, I want to thank my critique group—Peggy Christian, Jeanette Ingold, Hanneke Ippisch, Wendy Norgaard, and Bruce Weide, without whose help and support this book never would have been written.

Clarion Books
a Houghton Mifflin Company imprint
215 Park Avenue South, New York, NY 10003
Text copyright © 1995 by Dorothy Hinshaw Patent
Illustrations copyright © 1995 by Jared Taylor Williams

The illustrations for this book were executed in pencil with watercolor washes.
The text is set in 12/15-point Garamond.

Printed in the USA
Library of Congress Cataloging-in-Publication Data

Patent, Dorothy Hinshaw.
Return of the wolf / by Dorothy Hinshaw Patent ;
illustrated by Jared Taylor Williams.
p. cm.
Summary: Driven from their packs, two wolves meet, become companions, and form a new pack with their pups.
ISBN 0-395-72100-8
1. Wolves—Juvenile fiction. [1. Wolves—Fiction.] I. Williams, Jared Taylor, ill. II. Title.
PZ10.3.P245Re 1995
[Fic]—dc20 94-26798
CIP
AC

VB 10 9 8 7 6 5 4 3 2 1

For Bruce, Hanneke, Jeanette, Peggy, and Wendy.

⤙⤙Contents⤚⤚

RETURN

OF THE

WOLF

CHAPTER ONE

Lone Wolf

Sedra crept slowly toward her packmates, who were devouring the carcass of a freshly killed elk. Her tail was tucked between her legs, and she carried her head low. Her eyes focused intently on the torn flesh, and she hungered for a taste of it. Before she could take even one mouthful, two of the other wolves turned on her, biting and slashing at her flanks and shoulders. She instantly rolled over on her back and showed her vulnerable belly, but they didn't let up. Sedra quickly flipped back onto her feet and ran.

When she was safely away from the feeding pack, she turned and lay down on the soft snow that blanketed the meadow. She rested her dark muzzle between her outstretched front legs and focused her bright, yellow eyes on the other

1

wolves. She watched as they finished filling their bellies and as each found a comfortable spot to take a nap. She turned her head and used her long, pink tongue to lick away the blood oozing from a deep gash in her shoulder. Sedra was one wolf too many for the large pack. The other wolves would never accept her again, would not let her share in the kills. It had been too long since Sedra had eaten, and she realized she had no choice but to leave her family and go off on her own to find food. Her eyes gradually closed. Sedra drifted off into sleep, at last giving her mind and body a rest.

When Sedra awoke, the full moon was shining silver-bright on the snowy landscape. She rose slowly, her right shoulder stiff from its wound, and shook her thick, soft coat of blue-black fur, fluffing it out in the cold night air. She stretched and whined softly, then trotted slowly away from the pack. She did not look back. She skirted the rock pile at the meadow's edge and climbed the slope into the forest across from where the other wolves lay sleeping. She limped slightly, but the more she moved, the looser her stride became. She was on her own for the first time in her life.

⋖⋯⋗

Sedra didn't know where she was going, but she knew she had to go. She headed toward the boundary of the pack's territory, then turned south along

3

the edge, staying just inside her family's area. That way she would avoid a different wolf pack just to the east, who would surely chase her down and kill her if they found her in their territory.

The snow squeaked under Sedra's feet as she trotted along. Soon she happened upon an old logging road and followed it. When she came to a game trail crossing the road, she stopped, eyeing a row of deer tracks embedded in the snow. She plunged her muzzle into one of the depressions, eagerly sniffing. How fresh was the trail? Was the deer young or old? Male or female? Sick or healthy? As she lifted her muzzle from one print, she forced air noisily out of her nostrils to clear them before excitedly sniffing the next mark in the snow. She walked forward, tense, tail up, alert to the mixture of odors. The staccato rhythm of her breaths was the only sound breaking the snowy silence of the winter forest.

Sedra quickened her pace. The light breeze carried the scent of deer—a young buck—to her nostrils. She knew the animal was nearby. She stepped lightly, making no sound as she slipped through the trees along the trail. Tail down and neck stretched forward, she concentrated on the scent and scanned the brush for movement. Then she saw it—a brief flash of brown ahead where the trail turned near a stream bank.

Springing forward with all her power, Sedra dashed toward the deer. The buck spotted her immediately and leaped away down the trail. Sedra's long, smooth strides sped her forward. But the deer ran faster. Without hunting companions to head off the buck or to take over the chase as her body tired, Sedra didn't have a chance of catching the deer. But hunger drove her on, and she gave up the chase only when her lungs burned and her legs would no longer obey her will. She stopped. Her sides heaved as she sucked in gulps of air. Her heart pounded. After several minutes, Sedra turned and doubled back along the game trail to the old road. The chase had carried her into the neighboring pack's territory and she had to get out quickly, before her presence was discovered.

Farther along the road, Sedra's luck changed. The wind blew toward her, so the rabbit crossing the road didn't know a wolf was only a few feet away. One quick dash and Sedra's powerful jaws closed over the rabbit's neck, crushing its spine. She gobbled down her meal, biting off chunks and then jerking her head backward to swallow. Within moments, only the head, a few tufts of fur, and bloodstains on the snow were left. Sedra licked up the blood hungrily, then continued on her way.

‹‹·›·

In only a few hours Sedra had left her old territory behind. From then on, she picked her way carefully along wolf-pack territorial boundaries. If she sensed wolves nearby on one side, she slipped just far enough into the adjacent territory to feel safe.

As she traveled south, she fed mostly on rabbits. To keep her body nourished took three or four kills a day, and she wasn't always that successful. Mice and other small rodents served as occasional snacks, but they were too small to amount to much. Sedra was always hungry.

One extremely cold day, when all the other animals seemed to be holed up keeping warm, hunting was especially difficult. Her nose picked up no promising odors. She heard a strange, dull thump, a familiar sound, but one she had never before identified. Then she smelled deer. By now, Sedra knew better than to chase an alert young buck or doe. But this animal was close, and it might be bedded down where she could surprise it, or it could be old or sick.

Sedra focused completely on her sense of smell, stretching her nose upward and freezing in position as she deciphered the message on the wind. The scent told her of a buck in his prime, still musky from the mating season that had just ended. The smell of blood also tinted the air, so she knew the buck was in trouble.

Following the invisible trail, Sedra walked silently forward with her nose held high, quickening her pace as the odor intensified. She slowed again as she approached a clearing in the woods. Then she spotted movement and stopped in midstride. At the same instant, a new smell mingled with the scent of the deer. She had caught faint whiffs of it before in the woods. But this time, the aroma was strong and fresh.

Standing completely still, Sedra watched through the trees as the scene in front of her unfolded. The buck lay dead at the edge of the woods. A creature unlike any Sedra had ever seen before approached confidently, walking on only two legs. It bent over the buck, then reached out to touch him with one of its free front limbs. A flash of light glinted from the other front limb, and blood spilled from the buck's body as the strange creature opened its prey's belly and pulled out the internal organs.

Saliva dripped from Sedra's lips as she hungrily watched the strange creature at work. After gutting the buck, the predator quickly ran the shiny blade along the throat and inside lengths of the legs, pulling off the deer's pelt. Next, it removed the branched antlers and cut the meat from the bones. Then it gathered the meat together in a bundle, wrapped it in the pelt, put the antlers on top, and dragged the bundle off across the clearing.

Even after the creature disappeared and its scent had faded, Sedra stayed hidden within the woods. Things she didn't understand brought fear and caution. But the scent of deer was still strong, and she could see the dark gut pile lying on the blood-stained snow. A group of crows landed on the snow

7

and began pecking at the remains. Sedra's hunger finally got the best of her, and she inched slowly forward, flicking her eyes alertly as she reached the edge of the woods. She checked the air with her nose and scanned the clearing. Then she walked cautiously forward and sniffed at the gut pile. Sensing no danger, she bit into the soft mass and quickly filled her belly. She slipped back into the woods, carrying a leg bone in her mouth, found a protected snowy bed in a thicket, and fell asleep.

◄◄CHAPTER TWO►►
Jasper

The land was still gripped by cold and snowy winter when Jasper began to feel restless. Jasper was in his prime. His red-brown coat, marked with black accents, was thick and warm. On his face, where arcs of dark fur set off his bright, caramel-colored eyes and dipped between them, the fur was short and sleek. He had trouble keeping the tremendous energy of his strong, muscular body under control.

Recently, Jasper had been drawn to the female members of his pack. But every time he approached one of them, the stern pack leader Silvertip rushed over, snarling. As soon as he saw Silvertip approach in this threatening way, Jasper lowered his head and tail and turned away from the female wolf. With each day that passed, however, it became more and more difficult for Jasper to submit to Silvertip.

One crisp morning, Jasper found the scent of Sasha, the female leader of the pack, especially attractive. Silvertip was busy enforcing his rule over another young male at the time, so Jasper pranced up to Sasha, his raised tail gently waving and his ears pricked forward. When she saw Jasper approach, Sasha lifted her head and wagged her tail. Just as the two wolves were about to touch noses, Silvertip charged up with jaws wide open. He let out a deep growl, then clamped down hard on Jasper's muzzle. Jasper's patience snapped just as his rival let go. He pulled back from Silvertip, then lunged forward, slashing Silvertip's shoulder with his sharp canine teeth. Silvertip whirled around and grabbed Jasper by the throat. Jasper tried to pull free, but Silvertip's jaws closed down tightly on his windpipe.

Jasper sank to the ground on his back and gave out a feeble whine. He tucked his tail tightly between his legs and urinated submissively, wetting his belly. But Silvertip held on until Jasper almost lost consciousness. Then he released his grip and slashed Jasper's face. His teeth opened a long, scarlet gash. The blood flowed into Jasper's right eye as he lay helplessly on the ground. Silvertip stalked stiffly away, hackles up and tail held high, glancing left and right at the other pack members as if daring them to challenge him as Jasper had done.

Jasper lay panting on his side for several minutes while he recovered his breath. Then he struggled to his feet and watched Silvertip walk over to Sasha and lick her face. As Jasper walked unsteadily by, Silvertip growled loudly and lunged forward. Jasper had challenged the leader and lost. He could no longer stay in the pack. Without looking back, Jasper turned and walked away, blinking to clear his right eye of blood. Not stopping to rest, he headed south through the forests that cloaked the bases of the snowy, granite mountains. He would put as much distance as possible between himself and Silvertip.

CHAPTER THREE

The Meeting

As Sedra continued to move south, she fed on rabbits and an occasional gut pile. Once she managed to kill an old deer weakened by the long, cold winter. Her body became lean and strong. After some time, Sedra lost the scent of other wolves. She slowed her pace of travel, since no pack could threaten her anymore. The days grew longer, and soon the snow began to melt. Sedra spent more and more time in one place before moving on. When she found an area crisscrossed by game trails near a wide river, she decided to settle down. A big meadow broke up the forest of tall pine and spruce to the south, and a stream provided abundant water and an occasional duck or fish for food.

By the time the grasses turned green, Sedra knew her new territory well. The big river bounded it on the east, and an old logging road formed a clear border to the north and west. The land was open to the south, but she tended not to stray beyond the open meadow. She regularly marked her territory, lifting her leg and urinating on rocks and tree trunks along the boundaries, even though her markings were never answered by those of other wolves. Now and then she howled into the empty night, but heard no response. She was still alone—not only a lone wolf, but seemingly the only wolf for miles in every direction.

As she crossed the meadow one day, Sedra stumbled upon an animal lying motionless in the brush. She poked its spotted red-brown coat with her muzzle. It didn't respond. When she nosed it again, the fawn panicked, jumped up, and ran, bleating loudly. Sedra caught up in two bounds and sank her teeth into the fawn's neck. Her prey went limp, and Sedra began to feed. Her ears heard the bark of a doe and she glimpsed the fawn's mother approaching, too late to protect her offspring. From then on, Sedra checked the nearby brush carefully for prey when she spotted a doe on the meadow.

One moonlit evening, Sedra was tracking the scent of a woodland rabbit through the underbrush. The fresh trail made her salivate at the thought of warm meat. Suddenly her whole body froze. She strained her ears to make certain she had really heard the sound—the howl of another wolf, rising, pausing, and falling again, far in the distance. It had been so faint, and her attention had been elsewhere. She listened intently for another minute but heard only the hooting of a great horned owl and the wind rustling in the trees. She lowered her ears and returned to her task, nosing along the ground, following the scent of the rabbit. Sedra's prey had escaped while she was distracted. The tracks ended at a burrow, and Sedra turned away, still hungry.

◄‹‥›►

Sedra's ears picked up the howling again a few days later as she rested in the shade of an old spruce. It was unmistakable this time. Even though far away, the low, melodious tone rose clearly, held a sweet, high note for a moment, then slid down the scale, gradually melting into the murmur of the nearby creek. It was the same howl she'd barely heard before. Sedra rose to her feet, every muscle tense. Another wolf existed within howling distance, the first she'd heard for months. She panted in excitement. She had enough to eat in this bountiful land, but she had badly missed the give-and-take of companionship with her own kind, the physical interaction of playful sparring and gentle snuggling.

But what did the howl mean? Was a pack moving in nearby? If so, would the wolves be friendly or hostile? Sedra didn't know what to do. Should she answer the howl? Or was it better to remain silent? She stood there for a long time, listening for more but hearing nothing. Then she made up her mind. The sound had come from the north. She trotted quickly in that direction, moving with springy, ground-covering strides to the northern border of her territory. Starting at the corner by the river, she worked her way slowly along the edge of the old road, adding fresh urine to her territorial markers to show that a wolf lived here already, that this was her home.

The next day, Sedra was following a slightly stale rabbit trail. As she came to the road, she stopped in her tracks, her eyes wide with surprise and confusion. There, only a few yards away, stood Jasper. Tail held high and ears pricked forward, he stood in the attitude of a dominant wolf. Sedra's heart pounded with a mixture of excitement and fear. She hesitated for a moment, then dropped down and flattened her body against the ground with her head stretched out in front. Slowly, she inched across the road toward the new wolf.

Jasper walked stiffly forward. As he caught her soft, warm scent, he lowered his head, reaching his nose out and slowly wagging his tail. Sedra rose to her feet. Her tail responded to his, sweeping back and forth excitedly against the backs of her legs. Their noses touched as they sniffed intensely, blowing air out and then sucking it in again, each drinking in the rich aroma of the other wolf. Soon they stood nose-to-tail, still sniffing. Jasper stepped away slightly and placed a front paw on Sedra's back. He

arched his neck and wagged his tail energetically. Sedra responded with a play bow, flattening her front legs on the ground, keeping her rump up high. Then she jumped forward, and nipped softly at his muzzle. They dashed off on a joyful chase, tumbling along the road together, tripping each other and rolling in the dust. They twisted to their feet and rose on their hind legs, mouths open as they jaw-wrestled. They parted, panting heavily, then trotted side by side into Sedra's territory.

⊰⊱CHAPTER FOUR⊱⊰
Danger

From then on, Sedra and Jasper were constant companions. They hunted as a team, bringing down a variety of prey by working together. As time passed, the bright green meadow turned to gold. The wolves romped through the meadow, leaping into the air to snap at the red-winged grasshoppers that flew up. One wolf would dig at the entrance of a gopher burrow while the other ranged a few feet away, checking the burrow's other entrances to nab the rodent if it panicked and tried to run. Then they traded places. When they tired of gophers, they sauntered over to the edge of the pinewoods and curled up on the soft needles under a tree, their backs touching as they slept.

The nights became cold and frosty, and both wolves began to grow lush, winter coats. A gleaming mantle of long, gray fur spread across Sedra's shoulders, accenting the thick, black underfur. As Jasper's coat grew, its black accents became more intense, and the red fur behind his ears took on more color. Food was harder to come by. The fawns and elk calves had grown strong and swift, and the adult prey animals were sleek and well fed. Jasper and Sedra sometimes went hungry.

The first snow came, softly drifting through the trees and gently swirling over the meadow. It blotted out the contours of the land and turned everything into a stark world where the dark trees stood in sharp contrast to the whiteness of the snow. The snow triggered Sedra's memory, bringing back images of the generous gut piles that had helped sustain her through that last lonely winter. She became restless to travel in search of the remembered food. But her mate wouldn't join her. He stayed in the vicinity of the familiar meadow where he could at least track rabbits in the brush and capture mice as they scurried through their tunnels under the layers of snow.

One day Sedra went hunting on her own. She followed the creek upward, remembering she'd found food before around the edges of high meadows. Suddenly, she stopped. She smelled meat. She pointed her nose straight up and sniffed. Swinging her head back and forth, she pinpointed the direction of the delicious aroma. It came from the other side of the creek.

Sedra leaped across the trickling water and tracked along the slope. Her steps quickened as the scent got stronger. She dug furiously into the snow beside a large rock. She was just about to plunge her muzzle into the snow when she heard a loud twang, then felt a searing pain in her right front paw. Hunger turned to panic as she pulled back and tried to run. She couldn't get away—a giant pair of metal jaws, anchored to a tree, gripped her paw. She lunged and struggled, leaped from side to side and twisted her body in the air, but she couldn't break free. Exhausted, she lay on the snow, panting. Blood from her trapped foot stained the snow scarlet.

Sedra drifted into sleep. Day became night. In the distance, the howl of a wolf hung in the air as Jasper called to her. Sedra moaned softly and stirred, but she couldn't awaken to answer. All night, the howls continued; all night, Sedra lay helpless.

The next morning, Sedra woke slowly, feeling confused. During the darkness, her body had regained some of its strength. But when she tried to get up, her foot pulled against the trap chain. She fought back the mounting fear—she had learned that struggling would get her nowhere. Her foot, caught by the two middle toes, was numb. Sedra began to gnaw at the trapped toes. Pain shot up her leg, but she didn't stop. Sedra fought against the pain and dizziness. She couldn't stand to be trapped any longer. She had to get free.

Jasper began to search at dawn. Sedra hadn't answered his calls and she hadn't returned. He knew she was out there somewhere. He trotted this way and that, nose to the ground, seeking out her freshest scent. Now and then, he raised his head, nose pointed upward, trying to catch a whiff of her on the breeze.

Finally, he found her trail where it led up along the creek. But that wasn't all he smelled. Another odor drifted from across the stream. It was a scent that made him nervous. It brought flashes of fear, along with images of blood on the snow and memories of loud, booming noises. Jasper quickened his pace as he headed up the creekbed.

A flicker of movement caught his eye. He froze in his tracks and turned his head, following the figure that trudged heavily through the snow on the opposite slope. The thick brush partially blocked his view, but he could make out a two-legged figure with a long stick pointing up from one side and what looked like a hump on its back. Jasper focused in on the hump and saw it was a mass of furs—pale furs and dark ones. He quietly slipped up the slope into the woods and began to run. His mate was somewhere nearby. He had to find her fast.

Jasper soon reached the place where Sedra's trail crossed the creek. Her strong scent filled his nose with every puff of the breeze, mixed with the odors of blood and meat. Jasper's heart beat faster. He leaped over the water and bounded up the slope on the other side.

There lay Sedra next to the cold, pointed teeth of the steel trap. A dark red depression in the snow next to her wounded paw marked where her warm blood had melted the snow. She had gnawed herself free, but the effort, pain, and loss of blood had taken over, blotting out her consciousness.

Jasper whined and nosed her body. She didn't move. He pushed his nose into the snow under her chest, jostling her, but she didn't respond. He licked her face, drawing his long, warm tongue over her forehead, along the sides of her muzzle, and gently over her closed eyes. Her eyelashes flickered slightly and she moaned. Jasper poked at her body and whined urgently. She lifted her head and tried to wag her tail. Jasper ran toward the woods, then looped back and crouched next to her, poking her harder. He caught a whiff of the two-legged's scent and jabbed Sedra frantically with his muzzle.

Sedra roused herself slowly and struggled to get her three good legs under her body. She got to her feet awkwardly, holding her injured leg bent. Jasper dashed toward the woods, then back to Sedra. Using only three legs, Sedra tried to walk, then stumbled. She rose again and took a few uncertain steps as Jasper urged her on. Each stride got easier, and soon the pair moved silently and steadily through the woods. The odor of the two-legged faded until the fresh scent of pine was all the wolves could smell.

They circled across the hill from the creek, then descended back into the heart of their territory. Sedra collapsed into a protected depression at the base of a big ponderosa pine where she and Jasper often rested. Within minutes she was asleep. Her mate curled up with her, his side touching her back. While she slept, he stayed watchful. He raised his muzzle to check the wind every few minutes and glanced left and right to watch for any movement. As darkness fell, Jasper finally relaxed. He shifted slightly, lay his muzzle across Sedra's shoulder, and closed his eyes.

◄◄·►►

For many days, Jasper did all the hunting. He spent hours tracking rabbits and carrying food to Sedra while she healed. Her young body recovered quickly, but the pain made travel difficult. Gradually she learned how to step differently, now that she had only two toes on her right front foot.

One afternoon, Jasper hunted near the big river at the eastern edge of their territory. The wind shifted, bringing the scent of elk to his nostrils. He knew that healthy elk were beyond the hunting ability of a single wolf, but he felt compelled to investigate the strong, delicious scent. He trotted toward the riverbank, nose held high, following the powerful aroma. At the edge of the river, he found the source. A skinny, old bull elk lay at the edge of a willow thicket, unable to rise. One of its antlers had broken off, and blood dripped from a deep wound in its side. Jasper pounced and grabbed the elk's throat with his jaws, cutting off its labored breathing, and the elk died.

Jasper tore open the elk's abdomen and pulled out the stomach, intestines, and liver, and ate them. Then he bit into the meaty hindquarters. He filled his stomach with enough food to last for two days, then bit off a big chunk of meat and carried it back to Sedra. After she fed, he whined and nosed at her. She rose awkwardly and limped along behind him. By the time they reached the riverbank and the site of the kill, Sedra felt exhausted. But the smell of elk revived her, and she hobbled over to the carcass and tore off a few chunks of meat before crawling among the willows to sleep. Jasper dug around the edges of the carcass, loosening soil and snow that he tossed on top of the kill with his muzzle. Then he joined Sedra for a long nap.

The wolves fed on the elk for several days. By the time only bones remained, Sedra could walk with confidence and even run short distances. She and Jasper hunted together again. They would follow the trail of a rabbit into a thicket. Sedra would wait at the opening of the path into the brush while Jasper struggled toward her from the opposite side.

Sometimes the rabbit refused to budge. But just as often, the animal panicked and ran away from Jasper along the path, where Sedra could pounce on it. As winter deepened, the wolves sometimes managed to kill young deer bogged down in snowdrifts or old ones that didn't have the reserves to survive the season. Thanks to the casualties of the cold and the snow, the wolves were able to find enough to eat.

◄◄CHAPTER FIVE►►
The Wolf Pack

As the days became longer, the two wolves patrolled their territory more often. Sedra marked a tree trunk along the boundary first, her urine tinged with pink. Jasper sniffed intently at the spot. Soon she would be ready to mate. Then Jasper placed his mark beside hers, and the two wolves trotted on to the next rock or tree they used as a scent post.

During their courtship, Sedra would nip at Jasper, then turn her head and whine as she lay on her belly, her head stretched between her front paws and eyes closed. Jasper responded by cleaning one of her ears with his tongue. Next, he took the ear between his teeth and chewed it gently, over and over. Then he washed the other ear. Afterward, Sedra would return the favor, taking care of Jasper's ears.

Sedra often invited Jasper to play by bowing with her front legs down on the ground while she wagged her tail. They would jump at each other, placing their front feet in turn on each other's back. Then they'd roll side by side in the snow and end up with their backs touching while they lay panting. Each day they played and groomed each other more than the day before. Finally one afternoon, Jasper mounted Sedra from behind, his front legs holding her around the belly, and they mated.

⊰⊹⊱

The snow melted away and disappeared, and the sun warmed the earth. Sedra sniffed and pawed at the ground. The moist smell of the soil excited her, and she dug, intoxicated by the rich odors released from the loosened earth. Digging was more difficult now, since her right front paw had only the inside and outside toenails. That didn't stop her. She wandered here and there near the center of the territory, testing the exposed ground around the bases of the big trees.

Near the creek where she'd first heard Jasper's howl, she found an old fox den on the slope beneath an especially large pine. She sniffed eagerly at it, but the entrance was too small for her to pass through. Her paws flew as she enlarged the opening, a pile of dirt accumulating behind her. As soon as she could poke her head inside, she stretched out to smell the interior of the den. Soon the whole front half of her body was hidden, but she kept digging, pushing piles of soil out of the growing tunnel with her nose and paws. The tunnel sloped slightly upward, and she followed its path. When she reached the small enlargement at the end, she continued to dig until the tunnel was twice as long as her body from nose tip to rump. Then she dug a new chamber, a rounded cavity about two times the size of her own body.

She felt comfortable and safe inside her den, where it was cool and dark. Her body had become heavy and her belly swollen. She wanted to lie in the den more and more often, until one day she stayed for hours. Jasper whined to her from the entrance, but she ignored him.

The muscles of Sedra's uncomfortable body began to cramp. Suddenly, she sensed the need to push backward with all her strength. She strained at the effort. As the feeling passed, she felt her first pup emerge. She turned and nosed it, sniffing intently. The thin, moist covering that enshrouded it split, and the pup's quick, damp breath tickled Sedra's whiskers. She licked off the rest of the covering, chewed through the umbilical cord, and ate them. The wet, furry pup was wriggling weakly. It smelled wonderful to her. She licked it until the fur began to fluff up. Just as the pup started to whine and move its legs, the urge to push came again.

Several hours later, Sedra lay on her side in the

den. She was exhausted, but the pain and discomfort were gone. The enlarged teats on her belly tingled as one by one, four little mouths found them and began to suck their first milk. The life of a new wolf pack had begun.

-<-<-+->-

Sedra spent almost all of her time in the den, curled up with her pups, keeping them warm. She left only to drink from the nearby stream. If she went away for long, the pups whimpered and cried as their small bodies lost heat. Every day, Jasper brought food for her and dropped it at the den entrance. The sweet, wild scent of wolf pups filled the air of the den. At first, they slept almost constantly. After a long nap, their tiny, sharp claws prickled Sedra's skin when they crawled over her body, whining softly, nosing around for a teat. As the days passed, the pups grew fast. Soon they were walking shakily around the dark den, bumping into one another and tripping over Sedra's legs. Their eyes opened, and not long afterward, they were able to hear one another's whimpers and grunts.

One afternoon, a pup found the entrance tunnel and crawled through it to the outside world. The pup's eyes squinted at the bright light, and its nose sniffed hungrily at the new smells carried by the soft spring breeze. Within minutes, the other young wolves followed, with Sedra close behind.

Two of the pups—a male and a female—were black like Sedra. The third, a female, was colored like Jasper, while the fourth was a gray male. The pups waddled around, their plump bellies almost touching the ground. As their eyes got used to the light, they looked this way and that while their noses tested the scents of a new world.

Jasper trotted up, ears pricked forward, glancing from one puppy to the next. He lowered his muzzle to sniff the youngsters, and they all tumbled over to him, whining and licking at the corners of his mouth. He immediately regurgitated chunks of meat from an old deer he had killed. The pups licked at the meat and nibbled at the corners of the pieces with their tiny, sharp teeth. When they lost interest in the food, Sedra came over and quickly ate it all up. Then she lay down and the pups scrambled over to nurse. Jasper sat nearby, watching his family.

CHAPTER SIX

Selina and Ebony,
Tundra and Raven

From then on, Jasper and Sedra took turns hunting. The pups spent more and more time outside the den, romping in the sunshine and exploring. All four played together, pouncing on top of one another until they were a furry mass of tangled legs and squirming bodies. But as soon as a parent returned from a hunt, the giant fur ball instantly broke up into four little bodies, tiny tails wagging and voices yipping as they ran over to beg for food. They ate more and more meat every day and grew rapidly. Their blunt muzzles became longer and more pointed as the rest of their baby teeth came in. Their little, floppy ears grew into big, sturdy triangles that stood straight up from their heads.

The two female pups often played together.

Ebony, with her fuzzy black coat, would flatten her body against the ground, lying in wait. When her sister got close, Ebony would rush at her and pounce, trying to bite her neck with needle-like baby teeth. Ebony's sister, Selina, matched her father's quick temper as well as his appearance. The moment Ebony's mouth began to close down on her neck, Selina twisted her body with a whining snarl and grabbed Ebony by the throat. Then the two would tussle, rolling over and over as each tried to get the advantage.

At first the two young wolves were quite equal in these play fights. Selina would be on top, then Ebony, as they rolled in the dirt. But gradually, Selina became stronger. She was determined not to be dominated. Before long, every bout ended with Selina straddling Ebony, who lay on her back with her tail between her legs and her ears laid back, her pink belly exposed to the world. Then Selina stepped away, Ebony scrambled to her feet, and the two pups headed off together to explore.

-<-->-

One day the two females felt brave. They awoke from a long nap full of energy. As Selina led the way, they wandered off through the woods. A squirrel sat on the ground between the trees, its tail twitching nervously as it examined a pine cone held in its front paws. The little wolves stopped in their

35

tracks, eyes riveted on the squirrel. Then, slowly, they glided forward, stepping carefully with their oversized paws so as not to make a sound. Their movement caught the eye of the alert squirrel, who bolted for the nearest tree. The instant he took off, the young predators pursued at an awkward run.

The squirrel reached the tree with plenty of time to spare. He scampered out onto the first branch, using his long, bushy tail as a balancing pole. Then he sat down and chattered angrily at the pups from his safe perch. Ebony stood directly beneath the squirrel, looking up, while Selina headed straight for the tree. She placed her front paws as high as she could on the trunk and tried to get a grip with her sharp claws so she could climb up after the squirrel. Then the squirrel pulled a cone off the branch and dropped it, hitting Ebony right between the eyes. The little wolf ran off toward the den, yelping as she went.

As soon as they heard Ebony's pained cries, Jasper and Sedra jumped up from the ledge above the den where they had been resting and loped to meet her. They nosed her gently from head to tail, licking her here and there as they checked to make sure she was all right. Then they escorted her back to the mouth of the den where her brothers napped.

Selina hardly noticed her sister leave, despite the yelping. She was determined to get at the squirrel. She gave up trying to climb the tree and sat on the ground nearby, where she could see him clearly as

The bite on his tail threw Raven completely off balance and destroyed his concentration. His feet lost their grip, and he slid into the creek. The current pulled Raven rapidly downstream. He tried and tried to right his body and paddle to shore, but the swirling water kept him off balance, and his head was pulled under. Just as he managed to get his nose above water for a breath of air, his body hit a rock and under he went, water filling his nostrils.

Tundra ran along the edge of the stream, giving a sharp warning bark whenever his brother's head disappeared. Jasper was away hunting, but Sedra heard the barking and trotted over to the creek to check on the pups. Just as she reached the shore, Raven managed to get his footing in a shallow spot and struggle out of the water, coughing and sputtering. As his mother stretched out her muzzle to check him over, Raven planted all four feet and shook himself vigorously, raining water on both his mother and brother. Then the bedraggled little pup touched noses with the two other wolves, and all three headed back to the den together.

◄◄CHAPTER SEVEN►►
Growing Up

Jasper or Sedra often headed out to hunt just as the sun set, when the other parent and the pups were getting settled in the den for the night. The hunter returned in the morning, carrying food in stomach and jaws if the hunt was successful. After the family fed, they all took a midmorning nap.

One morning when everyone had awakened, Jasper and Sedra poked the pups with their noses, pushing them toward one of the trails leading away from the den. The older wolves trotted slowly along the trail with Sedra in the lead. Jasper looked back encouragingly at the pups. Selina trotted straight to the front and walked by Sedra's right shoulder, while Raven settled in between his mother and father. Tundra pranced along behind Sedra, nipping at her heels.

At first, Ebony stood alone, watching her family walk away through the forest. This was something completely new, and she was confused. Ebony whined, then let out a high-pitched baby howl. Jasper stopped and looked back at the unhappy pup, wagging his tail. Then he continued on his way, following the others around a bend in the trail. At the sight of her family disappearing into the forest, Ebony ran to catch up.

Before long, the trail widened into an old logging road and the forest thinned out. The sun shone brightly on the road, and tiny puffs of dust rose up as each wolf paw padded onto the dry surface. The pups had never been so far from the den. With each step forward, they became more wary. Selina tried to walk as close as she could to her mother's side, bumping against her leg awkwardly. Tundra was glancing all around him and sniffing the air carefully, soaking up the new smells. Soon all four pups were whimpering and letting out tiny howls of protest every few steps. They were so nervous that they forgot to watch where their feet were landing, and they staggered from side to side instead of walking in a straight line. But Sedra and Jasper ignored their complaints and trotted slowly down the road, heads low and tails slightly raised. The pups had to learn their way around their territory, and this was the only way.

Sedra turned down a narrow path through the woods. The breeze was blowing toward them, and soon the pups all had their noses lifted high in the air. They could smell the familiar scent of their den. Now they trotted more confidently along the trail, their eyes darting back and forth as they looked for the big tree that marked the den entrance. Soon they were back home. Jasper and Sedra lay down, but the pups romped excitedly. They chased one another around the tree and back the other way and pounced on the tip of their mother's tail as it gently brushed the ground. Then they settled down for a meal of warm milk before drifting off to sleep.

◄◄─►►

As the days passed, Sedra and Jasper took the pups on longer and longer walks, and the youngsters began to learn the way around their territory. They learned how to climb carefully over the rocks along the shore of the big river to the east without falling into the deep, swift water. They became familiar with the game trail that led up the hill next to the creek, where their mother had almost lost her life before they were born. They discovered the fun of running flat-out on the sunny southern meadow, where they didn't have to dodge trees or rocks in their path.

When they explored the boundary road to the north, they noticed the strong scent of their parents' urine and watched as Jasper raised his leg at each scent post, refreshing the territorial markings. The first time they visited the border of their territory, Tundra spotted the white flash of a deer's tail in the woods on the other side of the road and dashed off across it. Sedra gave a warning bark, but Tundra was gone, too excited to pay attention to his mother. The other pups crouched down, tails wagging, ready to run, but their parents growled at them. They glanced at one another with lowered eyes, then sat quietly on the road, ears and eyes focused in the direction Tundra had run.

A sharp bark rang out from the woods beyond, then another. Sedra and Jasper thrust their muzzles in the air and howled urgently and the pups joined in, their high-pitched tones rising, then descending above the deeper tones of the adults. Before their voices slid down to the lowest note, Tundra dashed out of the woods, tail between his legs, and skidded to a stop right under Sedra's nose. Then he rolled over on his back and licked her face. From among the trees across the road came more barking from the coyote that lived there. The coyote wouldn't face the wolves, but he made it clear that this was his family's home, and he would not welcome intruders.

-<--->-

One evening, after the pups were settled in a cozy pile inside the den, Sedra nosed each one gently, then walked out to join Jasper. Selina rose and followed her mother to the entrance. Sedra grasped the pup firmly in her teeth by the loose skin of her neck and carried her back inside. Sedra set her down with the other pups, then turned to leave. Selina started to get up again, but Sedra turned and gave a low, short growl, stopping Selina in her tracks. She anxiously watched her mother disappear through the entrance tunnel. Then she snuggled up to the other pups. Before long, Selina drifted off to sleep, comforted by the soft, warm bodies of her sister and brothers.

Jasper was waiting just outside the entrance for his mate. Now that the pups were old enough to be left alone for the night, hunting would be much easier, for the two wolves could hunt together. The bigger the pups grew, the more they ate, and it was becoming difficult for just one parent to bring back enough food for everyone.

Now there was more room in the den, and the youngsters' bodies lost touch as they shifted in sleep. When that happened to one of the pups, it would awaken and creep around until it found another furry pup to cuddle against. Then it would go back to sleep.

Once after awakening, Tundra sneaked through the den to the entrance. He looked out into the moonlit woods and let out a lonely little howl. Just then, a huge shadow passed right over the opening of the den, and Tundra flinched with fear. A great horned owl struck the ground with its sharp claws only a few feet in front of the den. The mouse he was homing in on had scampered away when it had heard Tundra's mournful howl, and the owl winged away with empty talons. Tundra turned around, tail between his legs, and crept back to the comfort of his sisters and brother, snuggling as close to them as he could before dropping off again to sleep.

When the pups awoke in the morning, they were still alone. One by one, they went to the entrance and looked around, but their parents were nowhere in sight. When it saw the empty world outside, each pup scurried back into the dark safety of the den and the security of the others' presence.

◄◄·►►

Just as the sun's bright rays began to penetrate through the trees, Jasper and Sedra appeared so silently that the pups didn't hear them until they were at the den. The young wolves tumbled through the entrance tunnel, tripping over one another in their haste and rolling out together to greet their mother and father. Big tails and small ones waved energetically as the youngsters whined and yipped and licked at their parents' faces. The hunters had surprised a young deer at the edge of the southern meadow. Both Sedra and Jasper carried plenty of food in their stomachs. Jasper also carried a front leg of the deer in his jaws. Soon all four pups were tearing away at generous chunks of

46

meat while the adults lay down nearby to watch. After eating, the pups joined their parents, lying with their bodies pressed up against them, so the open space in front of the den looked like a solid mass of wolf fur with legs pointing in all directions.

After they woke up from their nap, the pups continued gnawing on the deer leg, scraping off whatever meat they could get. Before long, they got into a tug-of-war, each of the four trying to pull the leg in a different direction. All the pups but Selina soon tired of the game and wandered off. While she was working on skin near the hoof, a magpie landed on the ground nearby. Selina was startled at first, but then she rushed at the bird with a tiny growl, guarding her treasure. The bird waited until the snarling pup was just inches away, then flapped its wings casually and landed a few feet farther off. Every time Selina returned her attention to the bone, the magpie hopped silently over and started pecking at the opposite end. And as soon as Selina noticed the bird and rushed threateningly forward, the magpie took to the air at the last moment. After a while, the pup gave up and ambled off to join the other pups as they chased and tussled nearby. Now that Selina was gone, the magpie settled down to feeding from the leg with its strong, sharp beak.

CHAPTER EIGHT

The Rendezvous Site

The pups grew fast with the food their parents brought back for them. Bit by bit, they had given up feeding on their mother's milk. Now they ate only meat. It became difficult to squeeze all their bodies into the earthen den. One afternoon, Jasper and Sedra nudged the pups into joining them on a walk. But instead of looping back to the den, the adults led the youngsters straight ahead to a new place, an area of open woods close to the southern meadow. A dip in the ground made a small bowl surrounded by trees, and a creek wandered through the meadow near the edge. After taking long drinks from the clear, cool water, Sedra and Jasper lay down, and the pups joined them.

As sunset approached, the big wolves got up, stretched, and shook the dust from their coats. The pups looked up at them, puzzled. They were far from the den, but Jasper and Sedra were ready to take off hunting. As their parents trotted away across the meadow, the youngsters huddled closer together. They didn't know what was happening, but they had become used to accepting changes in their lives.

From then on, the little bowl among the trees was the pups' home. While Sedra and Jasper hunted, the pups stayed at this rendezvous site, waiting for their next meal. When they weren't sleeping, they played and explored. They would take sips from the creek, then chase one another through the trees and across the edge of the meadow. The more they played, the more they learned about the meadow and what it had to offer.

The main channel of the creek was shallow and flowing, but trout darted about in the curves where the water was deeper and quieter. Selina stared intently at one of the fish, watching its every move. When it stopped moving for a moment, she pounced from shore, splashing into the creek with her front paws stretched out, trying to strike the fish. The more practice she had, the closer she got to catching a trout, but the fish was always too fast for her. Then one day she noticed a big trout swimming across the shallow center of the creek, trying to get from one deep hole to another. She pounced on it, and her claws sank into the fish's firm muscles. The slippery creature lashed its tail back and

forth, trying to get away. Selina was so surprised that she lost her footing and fell into the water, and the fish wriggled free. But the wolf quickly struggled back onto her feet and lunged again at the wounded trout as it tried to swim upstream. This time Selina was firm on her feet, and she bit down on the fish's head as soon as her paws got their grip. The fish flapped back and forth in her mouth, but it couldn't get away. Selina trotted out of the creek, her head and tail held high, with the trout gripped tightly between her jaws. She had made her first kill.

◄◄-►►

While Selina was busy trying to catch trout, the other pups were after easier fare. As they trotted through the long, drying blades of grass, dozens of grasshoppers leaped up. All a pup had to do was spring upward and snap its jaws in the right direction, and it had snagged a little tidbit. The three other pups spent just as much time jumping up after grasshoppers as Selina did in her determined stalking of fish.

But when they saw Selina's raised tail waving like a victory flag above the grass, the other pups ran over. They tried to nose the now-still trout, but their sister growled at them. She wouldn't let any of the others near her prize. She ripped open the fish's abdomen and quickly swallowed the guts. It took only two more bites to finish her meal. Then she headed back to the creek to search for another trout.

Raven followed his sister to the shore. Both wolves were startled as a big frog leaped in front of their noses and plunged into the creek. When the surface of the stream had smoothed over, Selina left to find another fish. But Raven kept staring at the water. He noticed a tiny puff of mud rise from the bottom. Without shifting his gaze, he leaped into the water, landing with both paws on the spot. He could feel the frog writhing underneath his pads. As he shifted his feet to try to get a grip on the slippery prey, the frog managed to wriggle free. But Raven followed the quick escape with his eyes and saw the telltale muddy puff where the frog landed. He crept slowly forward, focusing intently on the spot. He made a quick jump just as before, but this time he plunged his muzzle into the water immediately and got a grip on the struggling frog with his teeth before it could escape. In one gulp the frog was gone, and Raven began to walk along the shore of the creek, looking for more snacks.

The young wolves chased anything that moved. They saw that mice and ground squirrels escaped into burrows in the ground, and they dug at the burrow entrances in an effort to catch the rodents. One time when Selina was digging furiously at a ground squirrel's hole, Tundra noticed a flash of movement right under his nose and pounced without even thinking first. He caught a ground squirrel which had run out of another entrance to the burrow. From then on, Tundra stayed near Selina when she was digging. He circled slowly a few feet away from her, nose to the ground and eyes alert, looking for other holes in the ground. When he found one, he would stop moving and stare intently. Most of the time nothing happened. But just often enough to keep him at it, his patience was rewarded, and a panicky rodent ran right in front of his waiting paws.

◄◄CHAPTER NINE►►
The Wandering Wolves

After a day of practicing their hunting skills, the pups would rest in the shade of the big pines bordering the meadow. Only rarely did the skies turn dark and send raindrops down onto the land. The grass stalks had paled to tan, and the creek had shrunk to a trickle that flowed slowly between the deeper pools, now the only places where fish and frogs dwelled.

The young wolves were often hungry. The snacks the pups were able to snag for themselves couldn't satisfy the needs of their rapidly growing bodies, and sometimes Sedra and Jasper were gone for several days before returning with food for their family.

One evening after they had been gone longer than ever before, Sedra and Jasper returned to the meadow with their tails down and their tongues hanging out. The pups mobbed them as usual, licking the corners of their mouths energetically and whining in excitement. Nothing happened. The adults carried no food in their stomachs for their young. After wagging their tails and sniffing each pup thoroughly, Jasper and Sedra walked stiffly over to the stream and lapped water, gulp after gulp, from a pool. Then they lay down under the trees, closed their tired eyes, and went right to sleep. The youngsters curled up next to their parents, whining softly in hunger before joining them in slumber.

Just as the sky began to lighten, Sedra and Jasper awoke. They stood up slowly, breathed in the cold, crisp dawn air, and stretched. They poked the pups with their muzzles to awaken them. The young wolves came quickly to their feet, cocking their heads from side to side as their parents whimpered to them. Sedra and Jasper walked to the creek, looking over their shoulders and wagging their tails so that the pups followed. All the wolves took long drinks.

Again, the adults poked at the youngsters and wagged their tails. The pups responded by jumping excitedly onto one another and their parents, yapping and licking and wagging. After a few minutes of excitement, Jasper and Sedra trotted down a well-worn trail through the dry, brown grass. The young wolves hesitated at first. But the adults paused after a short distance, turned their heads and wagged their tails. The pups joined them. The pack had begun its wandering. From then on, the pack members would travel as one, searching together for the food that would allow them to survive.

<--->

The hungry wolves trotted single file along the narrow game trail, which sloped gently downward. The trail crossed tiny rivulets. Here and there, it intersected the main creek. At every crossing, the water was deeper and wider. As the land flattened out into an open, marshy area, Jasper and Sedra stopped. They raised their muzzles into the breeze and sniffed, swinging their heads back and forth, lifting their muzzles higher and higher. Suddenly Sedra froze in place, pointing her nose straight ahead as she pricked her ears forward and swept her intensely focused eyes over the swampy ground.

The other wolves followed her gaze and sniffed at the gentle puffs of air that drifted to them across the marsh. Each wolf lifted its tail in excitement as it caught the faint aroma of moose. Sedra crept forward, lifting her feet high and placing them down gently in slow motion. She worked her way silently toward a dense patch of willows at the marsh's edge. Jasper followed, while the pups stayed in place, flicking their eyes back and forth from their parents to the willows.

Sedra and Jasper circled to the right and disappeared behind the brush. The pups lowered their heads and stared intently, anxiously trying to catch a glimpse of their parents through the dense cover.

Suddenly the huge, dark form of a moose plunged through the willows, heading straight toward the pups as it splashed loudly across the marsh, sending sprays of water flying to all sides as its giant hooves struck the surface.

The young wolves stared in wide-eyed surprise, then scattered to either side as the moose thundered by. Jasper and Sedra ran behind, their long, powerful legs bringing them closer and closer to the prey with each stride. As their parents swept past them, the pups joined the chase. The moose crashed through the thick bushes until it came to a small clearing. It suddenly whirled around, lowering its antlers menacingly at the oncoming wolves. Sedra and Jasper thrust their front legs straight out and came to a quick stop in front of the moose. Tundra braked behind them and Ebony bumped into his body as she awkwardly tried to stop. Selina and Raven kept coming, overtaken with the excitement of the hunt and mindless of their parents' caution.

Selina swept around to the moose's right, while Raven went left. Selina sprang at the animal's flank. The moose shifted quickly to the left and gave a powerful kick with its hind leg. Selina's jaws missed their target, and the sharp edge of the moose's hoof grazed her side. The intense pain startled her, and

she tumbled into the grass. The moose spun around and rushed at the downed wolf. Raven saw his chance. He took a powerful leap and sank his shining, white teeth into the moose's rump. The animal bellowed and swung around again. The force of the sudden movement loosened Raven's grip and flung his body into the grass next to Selina. Selina regained her feet and snarled at the moose, who stood with lowered head, snorting at the two young wolves.

Raven got up quickly and turned to face the angry moose. The animal held its ground, jerking its head menacingly toward Selina and Raven and pawing at the ground with one front foot. The wolves retreated, glancing nervously over their shoulders, and trotted slowly back to join the rest of their family.

The other wolves had stood and watched tensely as Selina and Raven challenged the moose, not making a move to join them. As the moose faced the wolves with its head lowered in threat, the pack turned away and headed back toward the trail, parents in the lead.

When they reached a small clearing in the forest, the wolves lay down under the trees. Selina licked the blood from the matted fur on her side, then cleaned the wound with her tongue. The pain had already faded, but the memory of the moose's power would always remain strong.

➤➤ CHAPTER TEN ◄◄
The Struggle to Survive

The wolves spent the night in the clearing and awoke one by one just before dawn. They got up, stretched, and trotted slowly in single file along a trail leading northward. When they reached the northern border of their territory, the pups watched while Sedra and Jasper marked the boundaries.

Then a new hunt began. As the pups stood near-by, Jasper and Sedra spread out into the brush along the creekbed, lowering their muzzles to sniff the ground and raising them to test the wind. They both paused at the same moment, then stalked slowly and quietly through the brush. A sudden crashing sound startled the waiting pups. They saw a young deer dash through the woods opposite them as a big doe ran straight toward them, with Jasper and Sedra in pursuit. The youngsters tensed, ready to attack. Just as the doe was almost on top of them, she caught their scent and stopped in her tracks.

Selina and Ebony circled around the right side of the deer while Raven and Tundra faced her. Tundra ran toward the doe's left shoulder. She was ready for him. Her hoof shot out too fast for him to see and hit him right in the ribs as he leaped up. Tundra's body flew through the air, and he landed in the brush. Raven tried to attack from the other side while the deer was busy with Tundra. But she was too quick for him. She struck out hard and connected with his skull. With an agonized yelp, Raven collapsed in front of the deer.

By this time, Sedra and Jasper had caught up. But when they heard the young wolf's cry, they held off from attacking. Selina and Ebony followed their lead. The deer took advantage of the wolves' confusion, whirling around and dashing away through the brush. Selina took off after her.

◄◄─►►

Neither Raven nor Tundra could get up. Every time Tundra took air into his lungs, sharp pains stopped his breathing, so he could only draw short, slow breaths. Raven, meanwhile, just lay there. Sedra walked over to Tundra and poked him gently with her muzzle. He let out a sharp whimper, and she stepped back in surprise. She moved forward again, this time gently licking his face,

62

smoothing the soft fur with her warm tongue. Tundra relaxed, but he still could only breathe very carefully.

Jasper and Ebony trotted over to Raven. As Ebony delicately licked at the oozing blood on Raven's head, Jasper lay quietly down above his son, stretching his muzzle gently across his neck. Raven's father stayed with him, eyes watchfully staring straight ahead. Selina returned from her futile chase, her long, pink tongue hanging out of the side of her mouth, her breath making a rapid staccato sound. She lay down next to Tundra.

At dusk, Tundra was still asleep; so were Ebony and Selina. Raven still lay motionless. Jasper and Sedra awoke, stretched, and quietly slipped away into the forest to hunt. Ebony and Selina got up just as the dark night gave way to the first gray light of dawn and went over to sniff their brothers from nose to tail, their barely wagging tails brushing lightly against the grass.

Tundra stirred, then whined. He opened his eyes and ran his tongue around his lips. Then, with a yelp, he rolled from his side to his belly and lay there, panting. The sharpness of the pain had dulled into a constant ache. He was able to fill his lungs now, as long as he took the air in slowly. He took a careful deep breath, then rose to his feet as smoothly as possible. Pain ran through his ribs and made him gasp, but it subsided into the already familiar ache once he was on his feet. He walked very slowly over to the creek and lapped up mouthful after mouthful of the cool, clear water.

As the first rays of sunlight angled brightly through the trees, Sedra and Jasper returned with empty mouths and empty stomachs. Selina and Ebony trotted to greet them with wagging tails, while Tundra walked slowly, his limp tail barely waving. His parents sniffed him all over and licked at his ears. Then they went to Raven. The adult wolves lay down on either side of their motionless son, their heads stretched out over their front paws, each staring straight ahead at nothing.

◄◄··►►

The wolves kept resting under the trees, now and then dozing off into a light sleep. The sun burned down from the clear sky, making a patchwork of light and dark on the dry grass. A patch of hot light moved with the sun across the bodies of the wolves until it came to illuminate Raven's face. He did not move. Sedra nosed his body, but he didn't respond. His face was warm from the sun, but his body was cold. Jasper and Sedra circled Raven's body, poking and whining. He lay completely still. Finally, after one last look, the adult wolves turned away. They walked slowly to where the other pups were resting in the shade and nosed them. Selina and Ebony got right up. Tundra carefully planted his paws and rose stiffly to his feet. He stretched carefully, whimpering at the pain in his ribs. The three pups walked slowly to their brother's body and whined as they poked at it with their muzzles. There was no response. They turned reluctantly away to join their parents, who were already heading down the creek toward the marsh. The pack, now just five wolves, had to hunt again.

<-<-->->

The scent of moose was again in the air. Sedra and Jasper quietly crept into the brush while the pups waited. By now, the young wolves knew to spread out. Selina stood to the left of Ebony, and Tundra tucked himself behind a shrub to Ebony's right.

This time the loud sound didn't startle the pups as a young moose crashed straight toward them through the brush. When it saw Ebony, it stopped and lowered its head, snorting. Selina circled to the left. The moose saw her and kicked out with its hind leg. Selina waited, then sprang just as the kick ended. She locked her jaws firmly into the moose's right haunch, and the animal bellowed in pain. It tried to run, but couldn't get far with the wolf hanging on.

The moose didn't see Tundra behind the bush, but Tundra was ready. As the wounded animal struggled, Tundra leaped and grabbed its neck. His teeth sank in, and a gush of blood ran from the wound. Blood kept pouring out, and the moose fell to its knees, then collapsed. Sedra, Jasper, and Ebony trotted up to the still-warm body and ripped open the moose's abdomen. The wolves fed hungrily, filling their stomachs with chunks of the rich, dark meat. When they could eat no more, they walked slowly to a nearby clump of aspens.

Jasper raised his muzzle and began to howl—a mellow low note that slid gracefully up the scale, held a high tone, then subsided. As Jasper continued, Sedra joined in, her sweet alto blending seamlessly with Jasper's deeper voice. Selina yapped loudly, then broke into a howl, and the other pups followed. The five voices joined in a chorus of sound, rising, then falling again. The pack was singing the wild song of the forest, as wolves had done for thousands of years. Their music floated upward into the gathering dusk and spread across the landscape.

They had hunted together, and they had succeeded. The moose would feed them for several days. Then they would hunt again and again.

DOROTHY HINSHAW PATENT holds a Ph.D. in zoology from the University of California at Berkeley. She has written more than eighty books for children and young adults on wildlife and wildlife management, most recently *The American Alligator*. *Return of the Wolf* is her first work of fiction. In 1987, Dr. Patent received the Eva L. Gordon Award for Children's Science Literature for the body of her work. She and her husband, Gregory Patent, have two grown sons. They live in Missoula, Montana.